Jon
Scieszka

The Great Time
Warp Adventure

D1426176

PENGUIN BOOKS

PENGUIN BOOKS

Published by the Penguin Group
Penguin Books Ltd, 27 Wrights Lane, London w8 5tz, England
Penguin Books USA Inc., 375 Hudson Street, New York, New York 10014, USA
Penguin Books Australia Ltd, Ringwood, Victoria, Australia
Penguin Books Canada Ltd, 10 Alcorn Avenue, Toronto, Ontario, Canada m4v 3b2
Penguin Books (NZ) Ltd, 182–190 Wairau Road, Auckland 10, New Zealand

Penguin Books Ltd, Registered Offices: Harmondsworth, Middlesex, England

First published as *The Time Warp Trio: Knights of the Kitchen Table*
in the USA by Viking 1991
Published in Great Britain by Viking 1992
Published in Puffin Books 1993

This edition published in Penguin Books 1996
1 3 5 7 9 10 8 6 4 2

Set in 12.5/17pt Bembo Monotype
Typeset by Datix International Limited, Bungay, Suffolk
Printed in England by Clays Ltd, St Ives plc

One

'HALT, vile knaves. Prepare to die.'

'Is he talking to us?' asked Fred.

I looked around the small clearing. A dirt path went from one end to the other. Fred, Sam, and I stood at one end. A large guy on a black horse stood at the other. He was dressed from head to toe in black armour like you see in those books about knights and castles.

'I don't see any other vile knaves around,' I said.

Sam cleaned his glasses on his T-shirt and took another look at the end of the path. 'Yes, there is a Black Knight down there.'

The sun glinted off a very real, and very

sharp-looking sword hanging from the Black Knight's side.

'And, yes, he looks like he's planning to hurt us,' added Sam.

'Hey, it's not my fault,' I said. 'I told Fred not to open it.'

'You did not,' said Fred.

'Did, too.'

'Did not.'

'Did, too.'

'Excuse me, guys,' said Sam. 'Can we discuss this later? I think that large angry man in the black can is getting ready to kill us now.'

The Black Knight lowered his lance and set his shield in front of him.

'Um . . . Hello there, Mr Knight, sir,' I called across the clearing. 'My name is Joe. My

friends and I seem to have lost our way from

my birthday party. If you could just take us to the nearest phone –'

'None shall pass,' boomed the Black Knight.

'If you could just point the way toward New York we'll be on our way and –'

'None shall pass!'

'I think I heard that somewhere before,' said Sam.

'Thy tongue and garb art passing strange. Methinks thy band hails not from this shore.'

'What did he say?' asked Fred.

'He said we look funny, and we're probably not from around here,' I said. 'And right you are, Sir Knight,' I called across the clearing (I threw in that 'Sir' part because they always talk like that in knight books). 'We are not from around here. And we would just as soon get 3 out of here. So if you would just point that long sharp stick of yours –'

'Silence, infidels, or mayhap enchanters, in thy weird robes and boots.'

We looked at each other. We were all wearing jeans, T-shirts, and gym shoes.

We looked at the Black Knight. He had on pointed metal shoes, armoured trousers, an armoured coat with hinges at the elbows and shoulders, and a huge metal helmet that looked like a black bell, all topped off with a fluffy black feather. His horse was likewise done up in a black skirt, a black saddle big as an armchair, and a matching helmet thing with a fluffy black feather.

'Weird robes and boots?' said Sam. 'Look who's talking – the Tin Man with feathers. He even dresses his horse funny.'

4

'Enough of thy evil spells and chants, magicians. Prepare to die.'

'I think I liked "None shall pass" better than that "Prepare to die" stuff,' said Sam.

The Black Knight flipped down the visor on his helmet.

'Do something,' said Fred.

'Like what?' I said.

'Like . . . like . . . like, say some magic words!'

The Black Knight spurred his horse into a trot.

'Please? Thank you?'

'Not those magic words, you idiot. Real magic words. Like the ones your Uncle Joe uses.'

'Abracadabra?'

The horse picked up speed.

'Hocus-pocus!' I shouted. 'Eenie, meenie, mynie, mo!'

The Black Knight thundered toward us, his lance pointed directly at us.

We were about to be killed more than a thousand years before we were even born.

Two

BUT before the Black Knight arrives, maybe I should explain how three regular guys happened to find themselves facing death by shish-kebab.

It all started with my birthday party. My two best friends, Fred and Sam, were over at my house. We were just sitting around the kitchen table doing birthday kinds of things. You know – eating junk, drinking fizzy drinks, looking at the baseball my sister gave me.

My mum started scooping up wrapping paper to throw away. That's when Sam found the other present.

'Hey, Joe, here's one you missed.' Sam held

up a small rectangular present. It was wrapped in black and gold paper.

'Who's it from?'

My mum read the card and made a sour face. 'Your uncle Joe.'

'Yahoo!'

Uncle Joe was the best uncle anybody could have. He was a magician for a travelling circus. And his presents were always the best. Uncle Joe's stage name was 'Joe the Magnificent.' I was named after him. 'Before he went off the deep end,' my mother always added.

'The card says "Happy Birthday, Magician-in-training. Be careful what you wish for. You might get it."'

'This is weird paper,' said Sam, wiggling the 8 present back and forth in the light.

'I'll bet it's one of those disappearing coin trick boxes,' said Fred.

I took the present. 'Maybe it's a magic cape that can make things disappear.'

'That would have come in handy last year. You could have used it to make all of those rabbits disappear.' Mum still had her sour face on.

'Well, that wasn't really Uncle Joe's fault,' I said. 'I gave the hat the wrong command.'

'Come on, already. Open it,' said Fred.

I pulled back the black and gold paper and lifted it up.

'It's a . . . It's a . . .'

'Aw, it's just a book,' said Fred, rolling my baseball around the table.

And it was a book. But it wasn't like any book I had ever seen before. It was such a 9 dark, dark blue that it looked almost black, like the sky at night. It had gold stars and moons along the back edge, and twisting silver designs on the front and back that looked like writing from a long time ago.

I looked closer and read the title. '*The Book*.'

'Great name for a book,' said Sam.

Mum looked relieved.

'Hey, let me see.' Fred dropped the baseball on the kitchen table and grabbed *The Book* out of my hand.

'Wait a minute, Fred. Be careful.'

Fred opened *The Book*.

There was a picture of a guy on a black horse standing on a path at the edge of a small clearing. He was dressed from head to toe in
10 black armour like you see in those books

about knights and castles. He didn't look very happy.

'Oh, man,' said Fred. 'Wouldn't it be great to see knights and all that stuff for real?'

Wisps of pale green mist began to swirl around the kitchen chairs.

'Joseph Arthur! Close that book and stop that smoking this instant.'

I grabbed *The Book* and slammed it shut.

The mist rose over the table the stove, the refrigerator.

Mum and the kitchen disappeared.

And for just a second, I got that feeling you get when you dream you're falling. Then the mist and the feeling were gone. And Fred, Sam, and I were standing at the edge of the clearing. We stood at one end of a small path. At the other end stood the Black Knight.

Three

THE Black Knight thundered toward us, his lance pointed directly at us.

'Wait. I've got it,' said Fred. And he grabbed our arms and pulled us together. 'You guys stay close. On the count of three, Joe, you and Sam jump to the left. I'll jump to the right. One . . .'

The Black Knight was so close I could see the straps on his armour.

'Two . . .'

I could see the buckles on the straps.

'Three!'

We jumped. The Black Knight clanked by like a runaway train.

12 'Strike one,' said Sam.

Fred jumped back on the path. He stuck his thumbs in his ears and waggled his fingers, shouting, 'Nyah, nyah, you missed us. Nyah nyah, na nyah nyah.'

'Fred, are you nuts? What are you doing?' I yelled. 'Let's get out of here before he gets that horse turned around.'

'That's just what we want,' said Fred. 'He's too heavy and slow to hit us. We'll wear him out.' And then he yelled to the Black Knight, 'Come on, you big tin can. Give it another shot.'

Sam and I stood back on the path.

'Oh, great idea, Fred,' said Sam. 'He didn't kill us the first time, so let's give him another chance. I wonder if his mother ever told him it's not polite to point sharp things at other people?'

'Stand as men, you cursed knaves,' roared the Black Knight. He seemed even more unhappy than he was before.

'Yeah, yeah,' yelled Fred. 'Come and get us, Tin Man.'

The Black Knight yelled back, 'Prepare to die, foul-mouthed enchanters.'

'I know you are, but what am I?' said Sam.

'Same thing on three,' said Fred. 'One . . .'

The Black Knight trotted toward us.

'Two . . .'

We could hear his saddle squeaking, and his horse huffing and snorting.

'Three . . .'

We jumped. The lance whistled through nothing but air.

'Stee-rike two,' called Sam.

'One more ought to just about do it,' said

Fred, picking up a hefty stick. And then he yelled, 'Your mother was a sardine can.'

The Black Knight turned and raised his visor. He didn't look mad anymore. He looked positively crazy.

'Demon sorcerers. Foul wizards. Vanish not into the mists. Stand and die.'

'I really wish he would stop using that "D" word,' said Sam.

The Black Knight kicked his horse into a trot.

'One . . .'

He aimed his lance at us once more.

'Two . . .'

His horse stumbled and wheezed.

'Three!'

We jumped. The horse clomped slowly past us. The Black Knight waved his lance weakly 15 over our heads. Fred jumped up, swung his stick with all his might, and whacked the back of the Black Knight's helmet.

Booonnnggg!!!

The helmet rang like a thousand church bells.

The Black Knight sat up straight, wobbled, and then fell to the ground with an armoured crash. His horse stopped and lowered its head, sweating mightily and still gasping for air, but looking pretty relieved about dropping its heavyweight passenger.

'Going, going, gone! That one's outta here,' said Sam. 'Now let's do likewise before Mr Fun wakes up and starts with that "Prepare to die" stuff again.'

'No hurry now,' I said. 'With all that armour on, he won't be able to get up by himself when he does come to.'

Fred gave the fallen Black Knight another whack with his stick, and planted a gym shoe on his chest.

'All hail, Sir Fred,' I said. 'All hail, Sir – eek,' said Sam.

'Sir Eek?'

Sam pointed to the edge of the clearing.

Three more knights on horses, with swords drawn, were galloping down the path toward us.

Four

THE three knights charged. Ten feet away, they stopped. The lead knight, carrying a white shield with a red cross, raised a huge sword over his head and . . . and . . . and said, 'Hail, Sir Fred.'

'Hail, Sir Fred,' said the two knights behind him.

'Whew,' said Sam.

'Whew?' asked the tall knight with the red-cross shield.

'He means Whew and Greetings, Sir Knights. Are we glad to see you,' I said.

'Praise Jesu, but you sirs speak fair strange as thy dress. You must be of very strong magic to vanquish yon Black Knight with a mere oaken staff.'

The pile of armour wiggled a leg and moaned.

'For he hast slew many of our good knights of the Round Table.'

'For real? The Round Table?' I said.

'Aye. Know you of our Fellowship?'

'What did he say?' asked Fred.

'Have we ever heard of them,' I whispered. And then I answered, 'Are you kidding? King Arthur and all that stuff? Of course we've heard of you guys.'

'Kidding? Stuff? What sayeth he?' asked the red-cross knight's friend.

'Methinks they know of us,' whispered the tall one.

'Sure,' I said. 'I've read all about you guys – the sword in the stone, Lancelot and Guenevere, Merlin the Magician.'

'Read? Thou reads the written word as Merlin does?'

'Well, mostly *Daredevil*, Superman, and *X-Men*,' said Sam.

'X-Men?' asked the white knight's pal.

'Books of spells or fellow wizards, no doubt,' said the white knight. 'Faith, it must be a sign. You enchanters three have been sent to deliver us of our troubles. I am Sir Lancelot. These are my companions, Sir Percival and Sir Gawain.'

'Sir Lancelot?' I gasped. This guy was supposed to be the greatest knight who ever lived, except for maybe his son, Sir Galahad. And here he was, asking us to help him.

'Well, I am Joe . . . uh, Sir Joe the Magnificent,' I said, borrowing my uncle's stage name.

'These are my companions, Sir Fred the Awesome, and Sir Sam the, ummm . . . Sir Sam the Unusual.'

Sam gave me a nasty look.

'Welcome, enchanters. But we have not a moment to lose,' said Lancelot. 'Camelot is besieged by Smaug the Dragon from the West and by Bleob the Giant from the East. Mount behind us. We ride at once.'

'Huh?' said Fred, still striking a heroic pose on the Black Knight's chest.

'He said if we hitch a ride with them, we can go to King Arthur's castle and fight a dragon and a giant.'

'That's great,' said Sam. 'You invite us to a birthday party, almost get us run through by a Black Knight, and now you get us into a fight with a dragon and a giant. Remind me not to 21 come to any more of your parties, Sir Joe the Magnificent.'

We hopped on the horses behind Sir Lance-lot, Sir Percival, and Sir Gawain.

'But dragons and giants and things like that aren't for real,' said Fred.

'I didn't think the Knights of the Round Table were for real, either,' I said. 'But if they're not, who are we riding behind? And where are we going?'

Five

FRED, Sam, and I stood in the middle of the Great Hall of Camelot. Torches sputtered on stone walls that disappeared high in the darkness above. Knights and ladies dressed in robes and cloaks of all colours surrounded us. Dogs and little kids ran in and out of the crowd.

'Welcome, enchanters,' said a tall, serious-looking fellow. It had to be King Arthur. Who else would be wearing a crown and sitting on a throne in the middle of Camelot? 'Sir Lancelot tells me thou has rid us of that scourge, the Black Knight. How can we show our thanks?'

'Oh, thankest you, Your Honour, I mean Your Sire, Your Majesty,' I said in my best old-time English. 'That was mostly Sir Fred's work.'

Fred raised his stick and took a bow. The crowd *ooh*ed and *ahh*ed.

'Maybe you could help us out, King, sir, uh, Sire,' I said. 'See, we were in the middle of a birthday party at my house and we'd like to get back before the ice cream melts. Do you know the way to New York?'

King Arthur slid his crown back and scratched his head. 'York, yes. But New York, New York?'

'Yeah, that's it,' said Sam.

'Hmmm. The name ringeth no chimes. Merlin, knowest thou this place, New York?'

An old guy in a long blue-black robe and tall cone hat shuffled forward. He looked us over with flashing green eyes that gave me the willies.

'I know not New York. But methinks these three be poor enchanters who cannot find their own way home.'

The surrounding crowd murmured.

'Nasty old coot,' whispered Fred. 'Who asked him to butt in? Maybe I should just give him a whack with my stick before he gives us any more trouble.'

'Another great idea from the mind of Sir Fred,' whispered Sam. 'Hit the King's magician. I'm sure he won't mind. He'd probably reward us with a place to stay for the rest of our lives. A place like a dungeon, maybe.'

I could see we were losing the crowd. I had to do something, fast.

'Oh, we're enchanters all right,' I said. 'I am Sir Joe the Magnificent.'

The crowd *ahh*ed. We had them back.

'Would you show us some small spell of enchantment for our amusement, Sir Joe the Magnificent?' asked Merlin. And then he stood there, giving us one of those looks teachers give when they ask you a question they know you could never answer in a million years.

'Yes, please show us a spell,' said the lady sitting next to King Arthur. Queen Guenevere. How could I turn down the Queen?

'Spell, you say?' My palms got sweaty while I stalled for time, trying to think. 'Yes, a little spell.'

'Spells? Oh, yeah. Oh, sure,' said Sam. 'Sir Joe the Magnificent here is a regular magician.'

I thought of Uncle Joe.

'Magic? Of course. Bring me cards.'

The court jester brought a deck of cards with all sorts of crazy pictures on them. There were no suits or numbers that I could tell. Just a lot of strange pictures.

I shuffled the cards and pressed the deck to my forehead like the real Joe the Magnificent did at his shows. 'Yes, I am feeling the power of the cards, now. Could I have a volunteer from the audience?'

The Queen stepped forward. She stood right next to me and I thought I would faint, she was so beautiful. No wonder Lancelot was crazy about her.

I reshuffled the cards and tried to concentrate on the trick. 'Just a deck of cards. Nothing up my sleeve. Now you see 'em. 27

Now you don't.' I fanned out the deck face-down. 'Pick a card. Any card.' Sam groaned. Guenevere picked. 'Show everyone the card, please.' And while everyone looked at the Queen's card, I sneaked a peek at the card I would put right in front of hers. It was a guy hanging upside down.

'Now place it back in the deck. And I will have the cards speak to me, and tell me which one of them you picked.'

I carefully reshuffled the deck to keep the Hanged Man in front of Queen Guenevere's card. Then I muttered all of the magic words I could think of. 'Hocus-pocus. Presto, change-o. Open sesame. The cards are about to speak.' I flipped the cards slowly and made a big deal of listening to each one just like Uncle Joe

did. The crowd wasn't making a sound. I

flipped the Hanged Man. I flipped the next card, listened to it for an extra second, and then held it up. 'Your card, my lady.'

'The Magician card. 'Tis truth,' said Guenevere.

The crowd cheered.

Guenevere kissed me.

I turned to jelly.

'Faith, sir. A fair little trick,' croaked that killjoy, Merlin. 'But can thou do a true enchantment? A spell to change man to frog, or to vanish in thin air?'

The challenge hung there like a bad smell in a phone booth. The crowd went silent, waiting for our answer. Suddenly, a messenger burst through the doors at the far end of the Great Hall.

'Your Majesty! Your Majesty! Bleob the 29

Giant stands at the very castle door. He demands three fair damsels to eat instantly.'

King Arthur looked worried. The fair damsels in the crowd looked worse than that.

Another messenger dashed into the hall, nearly running over the first. 'Smaug the Dragon has been seen flying from the West. He will be at the castle walls in minutes.'

'Aha,' said Merlin with that evil-teacher voice and smile again. 'Here is a perfect test for our enchanters.'

'Go ahead and hit him with your stick, Fred,' said Sam. 'At least we'll be safe from giants and dragons down in the dungeon.'

Fred lifted his stick.

'No, no. We can't do that,' I said.

'What do you suggest we do, Mr Magnificent?' said Sam.

I looked at Merlin, then at Queen Guenevere.

'I think we should go find out if dragons and giants are for real.'

Six

NOW, you've probably read about giants in fairy tales. And you've probably seen giants in comic books and cartoons. But you haven't really experienced giants until you've met one up close. And once you've done that, believe me, you would be perfectly happy to never, ever meet another one.

I knew giants were big.

I had no idea they were so disgusting.

We stood on one side of the castle moat with King Arthur, Merlin, and the Knights of the Round Table. Bleob stood on the other. He was a terrifying sight. And an even more terrifying smell.

He towered at least twenty feet, wore no

clothes except two bloody ox hides tied around his waist, and hid the largest and ugliest face I have ever seen behind a crazy mess of black hair. Rotted bits of meat and bone, tree branches, giant drool, and cow manure drew a cloud of flies around his beard. If the sight of Bleob wasn't enough to make you cry, the smell of him definitely was.

For the first time in my life, I was speechless, and a bit dizzy.

'Make haste with the magic,' said Merlin. 'The foul air doth dull the senses.'

Sam nudged me and handed me a little stick he had split halfway down the middle. He and Fred had already clamped their noses with Sam's homemade clothes-pegs. I quickly did the same.

'Heddo, Misduh Giant,' I said, talking

through my plugged nose. 'How can we hep you?'

And do you know what he answered? Of course you don't, because you weren't there. Well, I'll tell you the truth. He belched. A long, loud, wet, noisy, and totally disgusting burp.

Sir Percival and the three knights closest to him raised their shields. They were too late, and took the full force of that awful blast. All four fainted dead away.

'Give Bleob three fair damsels to eat now, or Bleob smash castle,' said you-know-who.

And I almost hate to tell you what he did next. Let's just say that when he snorted, he knocked down two more knights with one 34 blow. And he didn't use a Kleenex.

Merlin gave us the hurry-up eye. I figured there was no way to stop this monster and was just about to yell, 'Every man for himself!' and run, when Sam stepped forward.

'Now just a minute, Mr Bleob,' said Sam, adjusting his glasses. 'You can't go around treating Knights of the Round Table like that.' He pointed to the pile of knights covered with green giant slime. 'We are three very powerful magicians who could wipe the floor with you if we wanted. But we're in a good mood today. So we've decided to give you a chance to have your wish come true. Right, fellow magicians?'

Fred and I looked at Sam, each other, and back at Sam again. We didn't have the faintest idea what he was talking about.

Bleob looked just as confused as we were.

'Right,' we said.

'Since you fairy-tale giants are always asking people riddles, we've decided to give you a chance to save your miserable skin by answering our riddle. If you answer the riddle, you can eat your fill of fair damsels. If you can't answer the riddle, you leave and never return. Okay?'

Bleob answered in a way too rude to describe. We grabbed our stick clothes-pegs and ducked. Ten brave knights fell like bowling pins, victims of gas warfare.

'I'll take that to mean "Yes,"' said Sam. 'So, for all the marbles – why did the giant wear red suspenders?'

'Why did giant wear red suspenders,' Bleob repeated slowly to himself. He raised an arm

to scratch his head, and unleashed a storm

of flies and a poisonous whirlwind of armpit odour that struck down another five knights.

'Because he . . . uh . . . because . . . duh . . . because red was giant's favourite colour!'

'*Bzzz*. Wrong,' said Sam. 'He wore red suspenders to hold his pants up. You lose. Goodbye.'

Bleob shook his head and scratched it again. Two fish heads and one rotten apple core fell out. Everyone held their breath. Bleob turned to go.

Fred and I clapped Sam on the back. We were just about to go razz Merlin when we heard the awful sound. It was another bone-rattling, teeth-chattering, giant . . . burp.

'Duh . . . hey. Wait a minute. You trick Bleob. Giants no wear suspenders.'

The angry giant turned and stomped back toward us. Even the trees shook.

'Bleob not like little peoples what trick him. Bleob crushes little peoples what trick him.'

Bleob stepped over the moat like it was a puddle. He raised one foot (which I won't even describe because it would spoil your appetite for a week) to crush us all.

Seven

WE all ran for the castle.

All of us, that is, except Sam.

Sir Sam the Unusual stood there with his arms folded across his chest, not moving an inch.

'Run for it, Sam,' yelled Fred.

The huge dirty foot started coming down.

'He's finally lost his mind,' I said. 'All of those bad jokes and riddles finally ate his brain.'

Sam checked his fingernails and said, 'Well, I guess the dragon was right. I should have believed what he told me about giants.'

The monster foot stopped in midair, one black and muddy big toe just inches from Sam's head.

'What dragon say about giants?'

'Oh, it really wasn't very nice. I don't think I should repeat it.'

Bleob stepped back. He got down on his hands and knees.

'Tell Bleob what dragon say about giants.' Sam leaned forward and spoke in a loud whisper. 'Don't tell him I told you, but he said giants are big weaklings.'

'No.'

'Yes. And he said giants are really just giant sissies who can only smash little tiny things like people.'

'No.'

'I'm not kidding. He said if you ever fought someone your own size, like a dragon, you would get your butt kicked.'

'No!' roared Bleob one more time. And

then he picked up two boulders, each as big as a car, and ground them to gravel with his bare hands. 'Giants stronger than anything. Crush dragons like that, too.'

Sam winked at us and jerked his head toward the other side of the castle.

'Why is he twitching?' asked Fred.

'Show Bleob dragon. Bleob show you how giant fight.'

'Show you a *dragon*, eh?' said Sam, jerking his head again.

Then I got what Sam wanted us to do.

'The dragon, Sir Sam!' I yelled. 'The dragon is approaching from the West!'

Bleob stood up, scratched his head, and burped. He didn't seem to know quite what to do.

'Well, what do you know?' said Sam. 'This 41

must be your lucky day. There's a dragon right on the other side of the castle. Here's your chance to show a dragon what a giant can do.'

Sam's idea sunk slowly into Bleob's thick skull. 'That good idea, little man. Bleob show dragon what giant can do.' And he charged off around the corner of the castle, knocking three trees and two huts flat, and shaking the ground for five miles in every direction.

Everyone still standing followed Bleob (not too closely) around the castle, just in time to see Smaug the Dragon gliding in for a landing. He was truly a terrible sight – big, ugly green head trailing wisps of smoke, shimmering metal scales, huge leather wings, coiling snake body, and iron claws.

42   Fred gasped, 'They *are* for real.'

Just as Smaug touched down, Bleob smashed into him.

'Sissy?' he belched. And then he clamped his long yellow teeth right on the dragon's snout.

Smaug dug his iron claws into Bleob's leg and thrashed his spiked tail. The two of them twisted up such a cloud of broken trees and flying earth that we couldn't see a thing.

We did hear how it happened, though. Bleob belched. Smaug flamed. And when giant gas met dragon flame, an explosion bigger than four Fourth of Julys knocked us off our feet and rocked the entire kingdom.

'Huzzah!' cried King Arthur and his sitting knights.

'What did they say?' asked Sam with a smile.

'That's hooray, Sir Sam. Nice magic work.'

We ducked under a castle arch to dodge the pieces of fried giant and dragon meat raining down.

'Thou has saved Camelot and the honour of the Round Table,' said King Arthur. 'Ask anything in my power, and it is yours.'

A giant toenail fell nearby with a thud.

'How about getting us back home?' said Sam. The last few small pieces splattered down outside in a gentle rain.

Fred and I nodded, wondering if we would ever see Home, Sweet normal, peaceful Home again.

Eight

'KEEP your eye on the ball,' yelled Fred. 'Choke up a little. Follow through. Meet the ball. Don't try to kill it. Just meet the ball. Ready?'

The stableboy looked completely confused. But he nodded yes, and gripped Fred's oak stick in a pretty good imitation of a batting stance.

Fred stood on a mound at the bottom of a tall, dark, stone tower connected to the castle wall.

'Okay, here's the pitch.' Fred lobbed our homemade baseball gently toward home plate. The stableboy swung as hard as he could . . . and missed by a mile.

I caught the ball and Sam yelled, 'Strike three! Yer out!' All of the boys cheered and began racing around the bases and yelling.

'One home run.'

'Babe Ruth.'

'Detroit Tigers.'

'Bo knows.'

Fred walked off the mound and met us at home plate. 'Do you think I didn't explain enough?'

'Methinks maybe you explained too much, Sir Fred,' said Sam.

The guys kept circling the bases, jumping and yelling as they crossed home plate.

'Full count.'

'Infield fly.'

'Suicide squeeze.'

46 'Oh, man,' said Fred. 'This is never going

to work. We have got to get out of here. This is like the Stone Age. Those guys at the banquet last night hadn't even heard of TV.'

'Gosh, what a surprise,' I said. 'Considering that TV won't be invented for another thousand years or so.'

'A thousand years?! I can't live without TV for a thousand years,' said Fred.

'And did you get a whiff of those people at the banquet?' asked Sam. 'I don't think the shower has been invented yet, either.'

'I don't know,' I said. 'I think the smell might have been coming from the food.'

The stableboys slowed down and sat on the grass around us.

'Ninth inning?'

'Ball four?'

'Kill the ump?'

'That's it, guys. Game over,' said Fred. Sam looked at the castle walls around us. 'No TV. No cheeseburgers. We are three 20th century guys time-warped into the Middle Ages. Score: Squires of the Round Table, 28; Time Warp Trio, 0.'

'Hey, nice name,' I said. 'Remind me to re-member it if we ever get out of here alive.'

'Speaking of which,' said Fred. 'How *do* we get out of here?'

I tossed our leather ball up and down. 'If somebody had let me read my magic book, I might know.'

'Oh, magic book, shmagic book,' said Fred. 'I barely touched your stupid book. And don't tell me we got here by magic. That only hap-48 pens in dorky books.'

Sam looked around again. The stableboys looked around with him. 'But if we did get here by magic . . . wouldn't we get back home the same way?'

'Exactly,' I said. 'So all we have to do is find someone who knows magic.'

We looked at the guys sitting around us. None looked particularly magical.

'Ah, forget that magic jazz,' said Fred. 'King Arthur said he'd make us Knights of the Round Table tonight. Let's do something useful while the sun is still up. Joe — you pitch. I'll hit. And tomorrow we'll explain how TV works.'

Sam rolled his eyes.

I walked out to the mound. Birds tweeted. The sun shone warmly. It was nice in Camelot, but Fred was right. We had to get out of the Middle Ages before we went 20th-century crazy.

Sam crouched behind the plate. 'Hum it, Joe.'

I wound up and fired my best fastball down the middle. Fred swung his oak bat and crushed it. The leather ball cleared the wall, still rising.

'Going, going . . .'

And then it disappeared through one of the tiny windows in the dark tower. We heard the crash of breaking glass. Three quick explosions rocked the tower. Red, blue, and yellow flames spit out the tower windows. The flames circled the tower, formed a cloud, and rained purple snakes, white stars, red dragons, and a hundred different weird and glowing shapes that dissolved as they hit the ground.

'Magic,' gasped Sam.

'Who dares disturb my work?' boomed a voice that filled the air.

'Merlin,' gasped the stableboys. And they were gone.

'*Omnia uber sub ubi*,' boomed the voice again. 'Show yourselves, demons of destruction, and feel the wrath of Merlin.'

The freaky cloud began to disappear.

Fred, Sam, and I looked at each other. We knew instantly what we had to do.

We ran.

Nine

FRED, Sam, and I knelt before King Arthur in the Great Hall. He couldn't get us home. So he figured the least he could do was make us Knights of the Round Table.

King Arthur tapped each of us on the shoulders with the flat of his sword, Excalibur. Queen Guenevere and the knights looked on.

'I hereby dub thee Knights of the Round Table. Rise, Sir Fred the Awesome. Rise, Sir Sam the Unusual. Rise, Sir Joe the Magnificent.'

The assembled knights raised their swords and cheered.

'Bring our newest knights their armour.'

Three squires staggered forward, loaded with swords, shields, and a coat of mail for each of us.

Fred's eyes lit up. 'Armour! Swords! This Middle Ages stuff might be okay after all.'

Then Merlin appeared. He was wearing his robe, whispering in King Arthur's ear, and holding our leather baseball.

'We're sunk now,' said Sam.

'He's history,' said Fred. 'If he even comes near us I'll run him through with my new sword.'

'Don't say anything,' I said. 'Pretend you never heard of baseball.'

King Arthur nodded. Merlin shuffled up and looked us over with those piercing green eyes once more.

'Ere since you enchanters arrived,' he said, 53

'I couldn't but think you were of a time or place I had not seen before.'

'Nope. We never heard of baseball before, either,' said Fred

Sam groaned. 'You dimwit. Why don't you just throw us in the dungeon yourself?'

'Shut up for a minute, you guys. Let Mr Merlin talk. He was . . . or *is* one of the greatest magicians who ever lived.'

Merlin bowed his thanks to me and continued.

'When this leathern sphere magically appeared to me this afternoon, I remembered. This sphere appears in a very old and very strange book. Even I know not whence this book came. Perhaps you know something of its secret.'

54   And with that, Merlin produced from his

robe a thin blue book; a book such a dark, dark blue that it looked black, like the sky at night. It had gold stars and moons along the back edge, and twisting silver designs on the front and back that looked like writing from a long time ago.

Before any of us could say a word, Merlin opened the book to a picture of three guys sitting around a kitchen table, looking at a baseball.

A familiar pale green mist began to swirl around the feet of Merlin, King Arthur, and Queen Guenevere.

Everyone *ooh*ed and *ahh*ed, thinking it was another magic trick.

Merlin smiled.

The mist rose, covering all.

Ten

'. . . AND Joseph Arthur, you can just march right outside with that smoke bomb and smoke yourself silly with these stupid magic tricks because I have had enough. Do you hear me?'

The mist slowly melted.

We were sitting back at the kitchen table as if we had never left.

Mum scooped up an armful of wrapping paper and stormed out of the room muttering, 'Joe the Magnificent, my foot. Hmmph. Joe the Brainless is more like it. Joe the Totally Irresponsible. A fog machine disguised as a book. Why, there ought to be a law. What 56 kind of gift is that to give to a young boy? . . .'

Neither Fred nor Sam nor I moved a muscle.

No one made a sound until I said, 'Merlin?'

'Black Knight,' answered Fred.

'Bleob and Smaug,' said Sam.

The three of us looked at each other. We looked at the book in my hand, the baseball on the table, then back at each other.

Fred shook his head. 'No way. That stuff couldn't be for real.'

'I'm not so sure,' said Sam, wiping the last of the mist off his glasses.

I wasn't so sure myself.

Then I put my hand in my pocket. I felt something and pulled it out. It was a card, a card from an old deck with all sorts of crazy pictures in it.

I held it up.

'Queen Guenevere's Magician card,' said Sam.

'Joe, promise us you're not going to wish for anything again,' said Fred.

I looked carefully at the twisted silver designs and the pattern of the gold stars and moons on the night blue book. For a split second it seemed like I could read what they said.

'I won't,' I promised. 'Well, at least not until I've read *The Book*.'

PENGUIN CHILDREN'S 60s

ALI BABA AND THE FORTY THIEVES • *Retold by N. J. Dawood*
THE AMAZING PIPPI LONGSTOCKING • *Astrid Lindgren*
ANNE AT GREEN GABLES • *L. M. Montgomery*
AT THE RIVER-GATES AND
OTHER SUPERNATURAL STORIES • *Philippa Pearce*
CLASSIC GHOST STORIES
CLASSIC NONSENSE VERSE
THE CLOCKWORK MOUSE • *Dick King-Smith*
DEAD MAN'S LANE • *Joan Aiken*
THE DRAGON ON THE ROOF • *Terry Jones*
FOUR GREAT GREEK MYTHS • *Roger Lancelyn Green*
THE GREAT MOUSE PLOT AND
OTHER TALES OF CHILDHOOD • *Roald Dahl*
THE GREAT TIME WARP ADVENTURE • *Jon Scieszka*
THE HOOLIGAN'S SHAMPOO • *Philip Ridley*
KEEP IT IN THE FAMILY • *Anne Fine*
KING ARTHUR'S COURT • *Roger Lancelyn Green*
THE LITTLE MERMAID AND
OTHER FAIRY TALES • *Hans Andersen (Translated by Naomi Lewis)*
LOST DOG AND OTHER STORIES • *Penelope Lively*
THE MIDNIGHT STORY • *Margaret Mahy*
MOOMINTROLLS AND FRIENDS • *Tove Jansson*
MRS PEPPERPOT TURNS DETECTIVE • *Alf Prøysen*
THE NIGHT TRAIN: STORIES IN PROSE AND VERSE • *Allan Ahlberg*
THE PIED PIPER OF HAMELIN AND OTHER CLASSIC STORIES IN VERSE
ROBIN HOOD AND HIS MERRY MEN • *Roger Lancelyn Green*
SHERLOCK HOLMES AND THE SPECKLED BAND • *Sir Arthur Conan Doyle*
SMACKING MY LIPS • *Michael Rosen*
TALES FROM ALICE IN WONDERLAND • *Lewis Carroll*
TALES FROM THE JUNGLE BOOK • *Rudyard Kipling*
THREE QUIRKY TAILS • *Paul Jennings*
TOM SAWYER'S PIRATE ADVENTURE • *Mark Twain*
TOM THUMB AND OTHER FAIRY TALES • *Jacob and Wilhelm Grimm*

Some other Puffin books by Jon Scieszka

THE TIME WARP TRIO (*with Lane Smith*) –
in reading order:

KNIGHTS OF THE KITCHEN TABLE
THE NOT-SO-JOLLY ROGER
THE GOOD, THE BAD, AND THE GOOFY
YOUR MOTHER WAS A NEANDERTHAL

Picture Books

THE FROG PRINCE CONTINUED
(*with Steve Johnson*)
THE STINKY CHEESE MAN (*with Lane Smith*)
THE TRUE STORY OF THE 3 LITTLE PIGS
(*with Lane Smith*)